But does Mr Mean spend any of his money?

Hardly a penny!

Guess what Mr Mean has for every meal?

A can of baked beans.

A can of cold baked beans because he is too mean to turn the cooker on!

Now, I am sure you are wondering how Mr Mean makes all his money.

He owns a factory that makes piggy banks.

And because Mr Mean is so mean he pays his staff hardly any money at all.

And they only get one day off a year! Christmas Day. Mr Mean considers this to be far too much time off!

If anyone complains, then Mr Mean points out his best worker, who has worked for him the longest, who has never complained and who always has a smile for his boss.

"Look at Mr Happy," says Mr Mean. "He works for me and he's happy!"

Late on Christmas Eve, after everyone but Mr Mean and Mr Happy had gone home, the factory received a visitor. It was Little Miss Sunshine. She was there to invite the two of them to Christmas lunch the following day.

"Christmas lunch!" spluttered Mr Mean. "What a lot of stuff and nonsense! Before I know it, you'll be expecting me to buy presents for everyone! Humbug!"

"How about you, Mr Happy?" asked Little Miss Sunshine, ignoring Mr Mean's outburst. "Would you like to come?"

"Oh . . . Oh I . . . I won't be able to make it," said Mr Happy. "But thank you for asking me."

"Never mind," said Little Miss Sunshine. "Have a good day and Happy Christmas to you both!"

"Bah, humbug," muttered Mr Mean, as he sat counting his money.

On his way home, Mr Happy looked in the shop windows.

"I wish I could go to Little Miss Sunshine's Christmas lunch," he murmured to himself, as he gazed at a bright window display full of presents. "But how can I possibly go when I cannot afford to take presents for everyone?"

With a heavy sigh, Mr Happy glumly trudged through the snow.

That evening, Mr Mean only had half a tin of cold baked beans because his factory was going to be closed for a whole day.

It was very cold in his house, but rather than light a fire, he went to bed.

Mr Mean counts coins rather than sheep to get himself to sleep. And while he slept, Mr Mean dreamed a very strange and troubling dream in which he met three people.

The first person he met was Mr Nosey, who showed Mr Mean what his past Christmas Day had been like.

Mr Mean saw himself sitting all alone. No friends, no presents, no comfortable fire and no Christmas lunch. And then Mr Mean saw everyone else enjoying themselves.

Mr Mean groaned in his sleep and turned restlessly under his thin blanket.

The next person to visit Mr Mean's dream was Little Miss Wise, and she showed him what the present Christmas Day was going to be like.

Mr Mean saw Mr Happy sitting alone and cold in his house eating a can of cold baked beans. And he doesn't even like baked beans. He was too poor to heat his house and too embarrassed to go to Little Miss Sunshine's house without presents for everyone.

"He doesn't look very happy, does he?" observed Little Miss Wise. "Not so much Mr Happy, more like Mr Sad."

Mr Mean moaned in his sleep and clutched his flat pillow.

The third person to appear in his dream was Little Miss Bossy. She showed Mr Mean what his future Christmases had in store.

A miserable-looking Mr Happy walked through the Town, and as this sad person greeted the people he met in the street, Mr Mean noticed something.

"Everyone is calling him Mr Sad!" exclaimed Mr Mean.

"That's because he is," explained Little Miss Bossy. "He isn't happy anymore so now everyone calls him Mr Sad. And that . . . is all your fault!"

With these words ringing in his ears, Mr Mean woke up with a start.

Sunlight was streaming into his cottage as he jumped out of bed.

"Oh my, oh my!" he cried as he rushed out of the door.

In a great flurry of activity, Mr Mean ran from shop to shop, pounding on doors and making the shopkeepers open up their shops for him.

C

Mr Happy was just getting up when he heard a loud knocking at his door. He could not believe his eyes when he opened it. Nor his ears.

"HAPPY CHRISTMAS!" cried Mr Mean. "No time to waste. Quick, quick, we're off to Little Miss Sunshine's!"

"But I can't go," blurted out Mr Happy. "I don't have any presents!"

"All taken care of!" cried Mr Mean.

And do you know what?

He was right. Behind him on the snowy path was a sledge laden with brightly wrapped presents.

Little Miss Sunshine was overjoyed to see the two of them.

Mr Happy and Mr Mean (rather to his surprise) had a wonderful day. Lots of friends, presents, a warm fire and a huge Christmas lunch.

"I couldn't ask for anything more," said Mr Happy. "Thank you, Mr Mean."

"You might not ask for anything more, but you're going to get it," said Mr Mean, and with this he gave Mr Happy a present. "It's just something to remember me by."

Mr Happy opened the present.

It was a tin of baked beans!